Treat the Earth well.
It was not given to us by our parents;
it was loaned to us by our children.

ancient proverb

For Isabella Andrea Grace ~ C F

For my grandmother, Tess Macnaughton ~ T M

LITTLE TIGER PRESS LTD,
an imprint of the Little Tiger Group,
1 Coda Studios, 189 Munster Road, London SW6 6AW
www.littletiger.co.uk

First published in Great Britain 2009
This edition published 2016

A CIP catalogue record for this book is available
from the British Library

Printed in China • LTP/1800/3447/0820

2 4 6 8 10 9 7 5 3

Where Snowflakes Fall

Claire Freedman   Tina Macnaughton

LiTTLE TiGER

LONDON

This Little Tiger book belongs to:

_____

_____

_____

The glittering ice world wakes up to the sun.
In this fragile white land, a new day's begun.

Snow leopards wake to the pink blush of dawn,
Still drowsy from sleep, they're cosy and warm.

Perched on the cliffs where it's craggy and steep,
Hungry for breakfast the puffin chicks cheep.

Far, far below, where the sea meets the shore,
Foamy white waves crash the rocks with a roar.

Deep from their den, polar bears tumble out.
On wobbly paws, they slither about.

Full of excitement they run and they chase,
In this most precious and beautiful place.

Baby whale glides through the crystal blue sea.
In the calm waters, he's happy and free.

Close to his mother's side, diving together,
Deep in the ocean that stretches forever.

Icicles glisten and glint in the light,
Silent, magnificent towers of white.

Drawn from their cave by the first rays of sun,
Lively young lemmings dart out to have fun.

Blue-shadowed snowfields lie still and serene,
Here where the air is so pure and so clean.

Sheltered by mountains, the caribou deer,
Rest by the stream, flowing icy and clear.

Off to explore, the small Arctic fox
Peeps from his lair in the snow-sparkled rocks.

Eyes full of wonder, he can't wait to go,
Nimble and light as the soft swirling snow.

Wings tipped with sunshine, the snow geese glide by.
They gracefully soar through the endless blue sky.

Calling each other, as onward they go,
Over the silent land, far, far below.

Frosty winds blow, little penguin stays snug,
All safe and sound in a feather-soft hug.

Wrapped in his mother's wings, sheltered and still,
Warm through the blizzard and harsh bitter chill.

Soft shadows fall as the sun slips away.
Snowy white clouds turn to purple and grey.

Arctic hares hop home, all tired and dozy.
Soon they'll be sleeping, and cuddled up cosy.

The Northern Lights shimmer and dance up on high.
Majestically, snowy owl swoops through the sky.

Over the magical ice world he flies,
And only the moon hears his soft, haunting cries.

Little seal lies in his mother's warm cuddle.
In the cold stillness, together they huddle.

The frosty land sparkles with softest starlight.
Sleep, precious ice world, sleep safely this night.